Anonymous

Poems by a Parson

Anonymous

Poems by a Parson

ISBN/EAN: 9783337398255

Printed in Europe, USA, Canada, Australia, Japan

Cover: Foto ©Andreas Hilbeck / pixelio.de

More available books at **www.hansebooks.com**

P O E M S

BY

A PARSON,

" Suavidicis potius quam multis versibus edam,
Parvus ut est cycni melior canor, ille gruum quam
Clamor, in aetheriis dispersus nubibus austri."

LUCRETIUS, IV., 998.

" Look here—
Gentlemen ; do not hurry on so fast.
And lose the chance of a good pennyworth.
I have a pack full of the choicest wares
Of every sort."

PEDLAR-WITCH, IN " FAUST."

LONDON:

HURST AND BLACKETT, PUBLISHERS,

13, GREAT MARLBOROUGH STREET.

1863.

DEDICATION.

TO ———

WILT thou look kindly on these waifs of Song.
That I have gathered from the fading time
When I was young?   With all their faults of rhyme
And reason, still receive them : do not wrong
My trust in thee, whom I have known so long
And loved so well, by bidding me withhold
This off'ring.   Were it music, such as rolled
When blind Demodocus entranced the throng,
'T were worthier of thee; but it would not bear
More truly to thee, than these simple words,
The message which no charm of liquid chords
Or subtle tongue tells fitly, that the heart
Hidden in the humblest gift transforms it fair
With Love and Beauty, far beyond all Art.

BY WAY OF PREFACE.

A FRIEND suggests that I should call the pieces
that follow, "Flowers offered at many Shrines."
I prefer, however, the title, "Poems by a Parson."
I don't mean to say that the verses *are* Poems, any
more than to affirm that the writer is a Parson:
but everybody knows that "apt alliteration's art-
ful aid" goes far to allure the purchaser of books;
and this help, you see, my title secures. My verses
are printed for a charitable end; and I beg my read-
ers to bear in mind that charity covereth "the mul-
titude of sins." I should think I need not deprecate
the wrath of the corps of critics. Unless there be

a Mr. Bumble in their ranks, none of them will so far forget himself as to quarrel with a foundling picked up in a Bazaar. So I send forth my humble volume, and say as Ovid said long ago about a volume of his—

> " Orba parente suo quicunque volumina tangis.
> His saltem vestra detur in urbe locus.
>
> .   .   .   .   .
>
> Quicquid in his igitur vitii rude carmen habebit,
> Emendaturus, si licuisset, eram."

MARCH. 1863.

CONTENTS.

	PAGE
BESIDE THE TWEED	1
BESIDE A HIDDEN SHORE	7
THE VIOLET	9
GONE	15
AFTER SORROW	20
THE RESULT	22
NORTH AND SOUTH	25
THE MAY	27
AT THE EXHIBITION	29
AUTUMNAL	32
THE LODGINGS	35
WHERE ARE YE NOW?	37
GLENDALOUGH AND THE FORGET-ME-NOT	40
THE GLEN	45
A REVERIE	47
REMINISCENCE	51
TO BLONDINE ON HER BIRTHDAY	54
TO EDITH	57

CONTENTS.

	PAGE
TO STELLA	59
TO A. M. D.	61
TO AMARYLLIS	63
TO A LADY REQUESTING LINES FOR AN ALBUM	66
SERENADE	68
MOSELLE	70
IN THE GARDENS OF HEIDELBERG CASTLE	72
COLOGNE	74
RHINE WINE	75
A VOICE FROM NAPLES UNDER BOMBA	77
EMIGRANTS' SONG	80
THE BONES OF BRUCE	82
DALHOUSIE	87
THE LEGEND OF S. JULIAN	92
THE CAUDINE FORKS	103
IN MEMORIAM M. H. M.	117
MORNING HYMN	119
EVENING HYMN	121

POEMS.

BESIDE THE TWEED.

My friend, you claim a long forsaken task.
And yet no task, when done for love of you :
How to refuse I know not ; what to write
I know as little ; for your mind is quick
To mark a flaw, and pierce an empty phrase
With keen intelligence—as is your heart
True, when touched truly—tender too, I think,
With no light sympathy, when once its chords
Are thrilled, but needing that its depths be stirred.
Ere it will answer,—as the Sacred Pool
We read of in the Evangel would not heal,
Until the Angel troubled it.

1   3

To-day
The Tweed's low ripple whispered in mine ear—
I passed by Melrose with its broken pile
Reared by Devotion, razed by frantic Zeal,
Each calling on its God,—to Abbotsford,
Sir Walter's fair creation—his last home.
Oft had I seen the place, and wandered there
In fancy,—now in fact I trod the courts—
An irreproachable lackey by my side,
With a perpetual and remorseless flow
Of catalogue and description from his lips,
Even in the room *He* died in.   When at last
Safe from his chatter—in a hazel copse
Hard by the Tweed that swept its banks below.
Thinking of that sad mansion—of this stream
With cold grey waters hurrying on, and there
Beyond, a railway gashing all the hill,
I scarce could deem 'twas Abbotsford and Tweed.
The actual scenes were poor and stript and chill
Compared with those my early dreams had loved
To dwell on.   This the legend-haunted Flood!
And that the wizard's dwelling!   Oh! no! no!
I'll keep the picture that my fancy drew—
The fair Ideal—let the Real pass.—

And is it not thus, often? Dwell we not
In two worlds far apart—the world of sense,
And that unrealized, wherein the heart
And spirit seek their portion? Which is real—
The Tweed and Abbotsford I saw, or those
I dreamed of long ago? Those yet shall perish:
The stone shall crumble, and the stream be lost
To distant æons; but my thought shall live,
Eternal as my life, it lives in me,—
The offspring of the spirit cannot die.
What is the Real then? Or is there aught
Within this visible world, on which the Soul
Can plant itself unshaken, and be strong?
Alas! I cannot tell: I look within,
And find nought there but my own changeful self
Reflecting changefully an outer light,—
Warmed or illumined by no inward flame.
Without—all changes, cheats, dissolves, decays:
Youth, Pleasure, Beauty—how like falling stars,
They gleam athwart our sky—to set for ever:
Faith, Honour, Goodness—names unheeded now,
And living only in the twilight dim
Of scarce remembered legend; Truth itself,
Uncertain as the flick'ring rays that play

Thro' rippling waters on a pebbly floor,
Discarded or denied. And what remains
To make life better than a dotard's dream,
And round it shed some living light of God,
Who—some say—is the Father of us all—
And others, Father only of a few?
Love? Love—the glory of the happy heart—
The mockery of the wretched—the Despair
Of those, perchance, who need its office most,
And most its tender ministries.
                                        To me
It comes not. Is it that I dwell apart,
Withdrawn to worship one fair Image—far
Too perfect for this Earth, idealized
From many a vision of a wayward heart
Inspiring restless Fancy—into one
As far above the real that exists,
As were the Dreamland Landscapes I had loved,
Above the actual Abbotsford and Tweed?
Gray Time fares on: around me throngs the world,
With all its Mystery and Strife; and I
Am in the midst of all—a part of all;
And yet, within my heart, in the deep core
And silent centre of the inner life,

Where uncompanioned ever dwells the Soul,
There is a void the world can never fill—
The void which Nature leaves that One may rear
Therein her golden throne—a void I fain
Would fill with that fair Image ; but ah me !
She comes not—nor in sooth will ever come ;
And when I fly from self, and eager seek
To trace her shadow in the work-day world,
And gaze around with waiting, searching eyes.
I meet the same stale bow, or smile, or jest,
The dull frivolities of hackneyed life,
And a blank stare, if on my moodier brow
Have Disappointment and Expectance writ
A deeper line of gloominess and care.
What matter, after all ? Do you believe,
Dear friend, that what I say is only true
Of me who say it—or of me at all ?
Is life not lonely—do not most hearts seek
(When hopeless ev'n, by Hope's strange glamour wiled.)
The One who could interpret all their strifes,
And know by keen electric sympathy
Their needs, and answer them—fulfil their love.
And stay their dark unrest ? And finding not
That which they crave, some (do they not ?) grow cold.

As I have known true hearts left vacant grow
Cold, hard, ay, selfish—till their bright spring bloom
Had turned to ashes—as full many must—
While man's high hopes and longings mock the lot
Assigned him in the sphere of mortal life,
That leads—ah! leave us still that Godlike hope
That leads to the Immortal.

BESIDE A HIDDEN SHORE.

THE bells in the darkness knelling—
  The lights on the hidden shore—
The land-breeze falling and swelling
  Thro' the pines on the headland hoar—

The long, slow heave of the ocean
  As it travels on to the strand—
The fitful and muffled motion
  And noise of life from the land—

All these, as my bark is sliding
  Along thro' the gloom of the night,
Reprove me with gentlest chiding,
  As the voice of a mother might.

7

BESIDE A HIDDEN SHORE.

In light and in music speaking
　With a measured and dreamful tone,
My heart, that is wearily seeking
　Release from its toil and moan,

They chide for its nerveless shrinking
　From watching and care and strife—
For its faithlessness ever thinking
　Of the toil, not the crown, of Life.

So the bells in their dim tower knelling,
　Winds and waves in their roar and roll,
Of Worship and Labour telling,
　Rebuke my unfaithful Soul.

THE VIOLET.

AFTER long shivering 'mid the frost and snow,
Their naked branches clanging in the wind
And in the chill rains dripping—the bleak woods
Begin to flush with tender green, and low
Amid their feathery boughs the Zephyr sighs,
Like the tired voice of one who long has pined
O'er a remembered sorrow. Solitudes
Are then no longer voiceless, but arise
Commingled melodies of birds and streams
And gentle airs—soft anthems to soft skies.
Nor incense is awanting, fragrant, rare,
As from the blending of a Seraph's breath,
With the low sigh of penitential prayer,
Up float Earth's odours—as in happy dreams

9

Lithe forms of shadowy loveliness enwreath
Their wavering outlines in the ivory gleams
That fairy moonshine sheds on dreamland air.
And 'mong the joyful sisterhood of flowers
That look with mild moist eyes to Heaven, and twine
Fresh garlands for the rosy-fingered Hours
That dance along the sunbeams, where the Pine
And knotty Oak and tasselled larch, and elm
Spread their wide arms—none blooms so softly fair,
In tint so pure—so rich beyond compare
In fragrance, like the winds from some far realm
Of fabled Elfland, where the wandering breeze
Is living music, and nepenthe mild
For all the ills that living things must bear—
How gay soe'er their being; none so sweet
In all its dewy freshness—the bright child
Of woodland beauty—darling of the trees
That watch it binding round their muffled feet
Its little velvet mat of shady blue
And damp dark green—none is in shape and hue
And odour lovely as the Violet—
The modest bud—as pure—as bright—as shy
As the quick glancing of a maiden's eye—
The loveliest gem in Spring's green coronet,

—

That with its smile responsive to the Sun,
Tells that the fount of winter's tears are dry,
And the blithe reign of jocund Spring begun.
Upon my heart long since there passed the chill
And blight of gloomy winter: many storms
Had tossed my spirit, and my laggard will
Rose not heroic 'gainst their dangerous sway;
And thro' the dismal winter-light sad forms
Unresting and remorseful ever thronged
Stern louring my dull sky by night and day.
My heart and soul and all my being longed
For light and rest and beauty. All my dreams
And thoughts and prayers and fancies bent to this.
As a frail spirit yearning for Heaven's bliss
Turns to the throne whence God's great mercy beams:
And one fair morning—ere the twilight gray
Was scattered by the Sunrise—when the bars
Of earthly life were lifted from the Soul,
And the weird influence of the golden stars
Thro' the dark spell of sleep, 'neath their control
Held all the subject powers of life and thought,—
Then was the thick veil of dull sense upraised,
And through a pale and mystic gleam I gazed,
And saw—ah, blessed vision! never hide.

Ye stars! the memory and the hope from me—
A dell so beauteous that the Idean grove,
Where the three Queens of Heaven the Shepherd sought
Were bleak beside it. The rich star of love
Shone with the full-orbed Moon in all her pride
Upon its plumy trees ; and the broad sea
With one white track of silver on its breast
Slumbered beyond—hushed in unmurmuring rest.
Methought I trod the dell, beneath the shade
Of the tall trees that chequered th' emerald lea
With dusky shadows ; and a vista oped
Before me in the lustrous light, and sloped
Up to a fount, whose rivulet sang and strayed—
A gleaming thread of life and light afar
Amid the woodlands ; and the morning star
Right down into the welling fountain shone
With silvery glitter. By the smooth, soft brink
Smiling mid golden moss, there bloomed alone
One fragrant violet. On my tranced ear
There breathed a voice—as from some distant sphere
Of chiming choirs, an Ellin strain had strayed—
"Stoop, pluck the violet ; of the fountain drink :
'Twill be thy heart's nepenthe, and the flower
The magic and the blessing of thy life."

The fairy voice was silent: I obeyed,
I drank, and all the freshness of an hour
When sorrow was a name unknown returned;
I plucked the flower, and to my bosom pressed
Its purple softness; and within my breast,
Where erst wild passion nursed its fieriest strife,
I felt a joyful and most holy calm—
As tho' my years of storm-beat change had earned
Refreshful rest at length and healing balm.
Then seemed the blessed vision all to fade,
And slumber left me; on the drowsy air
Were jangling loud the bells from the gray tower
That by the river rises; day's stern light
Came back unto me, and the Dreamland fair
Was gone,—but not for ever: for I made
A vow, as kneeling in that morning hour
I communed with the Spirit of the Past
And read the future in the vanished night.
I vowed that wheresoe'er my lot were cast
In years to come—amid the city's toil,
Or in the Desert's silence—by the shore
Of ocean, or of lake, by winding stream
In golden valley, or in sunlit plain,
In East or West—gay South, or Northland hoar—

No tame delay, no change, no joy, no pain
Should the deep purpose of my being foil,
To find the flower and fountain of my dream.
With them the well-spring of my life is hid:
I seek them now with long-expectant eyes;
O'er the strained eyeball droops the weary lid;
The way-worn steps are tottering, and the air
Is heavy: where the Dreamland valley lies
The moonlit ether sparkles sheen and light—
Springs the cool fount, and floats the fragrance rare
Of the sweet flower.   Upon my aching sight
When will that scene gleam 'neath its tranquil skies?
Where sleeps that valley 'neath Astarte's light?
Ah! gentle Ladye, canst thou tell me where?

GONE

SADLY falls the westering sunshine
　Round our silent home to-night ;
Sadly muse I in the chambers
　Whence our friends have ta'en their flight :
All around is still and empty—
　Only here and there I glean
Little waifs and strays that tell me
　Where the parted guests have been :
Little waifs and strays that whisper,
　With an accent low and sweet,
" Mingled here the happy voices,
　Twinkled here the fairy feet—
Rose and fell the merry laughter,
　Echoed here the darling song—"

15

Echoed! ah! the happy voices
  With me here shall echo long.
Evening comes; but while its shadows
  Droop around me dim and gray,
Memory pours along the landscape
  Purer light than light of Day.
There, the River lies before me
  In that calm and silvery eve,
And I hear the Angel music
  Round me its enchantment weave:
There again. the rainy meadow
  Beaten by the cloudy wind
Fret in front the whitening waters,
  Rise the frowning heights behind:
Yonder. yet again, the carriage
  Toiling up the mountain road,
Horse and man alike unconscious
  Of the value of their load;
Just as long ago at Mamre
  Abr'ham washing wearied feet
Reck'd not they that morn had trodden
  Far on high a golden street.
Other visions pass before me—
  Other scenes and sounds arise—

But no more I'll gaze and listen
  'Neath these sad and silent skies—
Tho' in every scene awakened
  By Remembrance' fatal spell.
Ever shine the same fair faces,
  Ever the same voices swell—
Ever the same group is gathered—
  Whitest light around them thrown,
And for them the Earth is fragrant,
  And its lap with flowers is strown.
Pass away, ye blessed visions—
  Such as ye have passed before :
Wherefore linger, when the spirits
  That inspired you—come no more?
Wherefore stay, like flower-wreathed arches,
  When the pageant's past and gone—
Like the festal lamps, when vanished
  Is the light that in them shone?
'Twere not well that ye should linger,
  And so pure and bright intrude
On the hours of life's long labour,
  On the spirit's solitude.
Oh ! away ! too fair and happy—
  Duller scenes must intervene—

17   c

GONE.

Fade into a deeper distance,
    Unforgotten—but unseen,
Rise not with so keen a brightness--
    Else mine eye must dim with tears
The effulgence of the beauty
    That my spirit loves, yet fears.
Pass away—but take the blessing
    Of a heart that ye have blest,
That perchance when sad and weary
    In the thought of you shalt rest:
That, when in a world of falseness,
    Tost with doubt and tried with wrong,
From your memory shall gather
    Hope more bright and faith more strong.
Yes! I ofttimes shall recall ye—
    Happy group and joyous hours,
Vocal with that spirit music,
    Garlanded with fadeless flowers;
But, oh linger not beside me,
    Leave me uncompanioned now;
Voices from the future call me,
    " Child, why thus a troubled brow,
Gaze not back on flowers and sunshine:
    List not to the gentlest song;

18

—

Take the light and strength they give thee.
Onward, then—be brave and strong."
Rise not then so fair and witching ;
   Why should I obscure with tears
The effulgence and the glory
   That my spirit loves. yet fears :
Shall I not recall their brightness
   With a blessing all my years !

AFTER SORROW.

I LOOK back to the shades of vanished years;
I scarce could see them once—so bright the rays
Of sunshine gilding them ; now blinding tears
Dim all that morning landscape, like a haze.
It is not changed : ah no! the peaceful lake
Still smiles amidst its mountains, and the breeze
Scented with heather sweeps o'er moor and brake—
Still 'mong the wild flowers hum the nimble bees ;
Still stands the quaint old church—the ivy leaf
A little higher on the wall has crept ;
Still falls the shadow, like a cloak of grief,
O'er the green mounds where love bereaved has wept ;
Still sinks the ruddy sun in summer eve
Behind the empurpled mountains as of yore.

20

AFTER SORROW.

Still the grey fields the twilight dews receive,
Still all is fair; but on my heart no more
Falls spring's soft shower of love—or summer's ray
Of kindly warmth—or Autumn's genial glow:
But only Winter with its cheerless day,
And its long darkness and its driving snow.

THE RESULT.

I might have seen disaster ere it came :
   I might have known the Eden would not last—
That my dark destiny with sword of flame
   Would drive me from it : and the portal passed.
'Tis barred for ever ; I may come no more—
Life lies discrownéd now—the life of life is o'er.

When last I loved, thro' many a haunted night
   My heart's lone anguish paid the penance due
To Love unworthy and insulted Right.
   Till of repentance, consolation grew,
And I could gather from my pain at length
A wise experience and a stable strength.

But what can solace now or strength afford?
   Will it bring peace to curse the hapless hour
When first I saw thee—beautiful—adored?
   Or shall I bless it? Ah! I lack the power
To do or one or other: all I know
Is that it bared my breast to love and keenest woe.

I saw thee—lovely as the dawn: I heard
   Thy voice—the music of each young day-dream:
Ah! how my heart laid up thy lightest word;
   Ah! how my memory dwelt on every beam
Of that blue eye, which like an inner light
Shone in my heart, the while it blest my sight!

And did I love thee? Does the gushing rill,
   When Winter bleak unclasps his icy hand,
Bound to the lake that sleeps below the hill!
   Do violets bloom when Spring breathes o'er the land?
I loved, as men will love—nor till too late
Saw between me and thee the barrier of Fate.

And now—my lesson? I must not rebel—
   I must not weary of a weary life—
And tho' my heart should burn—a secret Hell—
   Must smoothe my brow, nor show the wasting strife:

must not raise to Heaven an angry eye—
And mock the madd'ning calm of that eternal sky.

I had forgot: no titled wealth was mine:
    What a dull fool! to deem a human heart
An off'ring meet for Love and Beauty's shrine:
    How much I need to learn of the world's art!
And if the teaching seem a little rough
And painful, yet 'tis plain and positive enough.

I shall not need to have it o'er again,
    Nor curb once more my stubborn will and pride;
My heart deep stabbed has bled, and not in vain ;
    It will be wise in future, and will chide
Into subjection its vagaries wild—
As a smooth matron checks a wilful child.

Then hush, dark heart! why storm, and heave, and swell?
    After the tempest comes the dull deep rest :
What! art thou wayward yet ?   My love, farewell!
    I dreamed I might have dreamed upon thy breast :
The cold world's voice broke that dear dream; and see,
I tread night-paths, and leave my Light and Hope with
    Thee.

NORTH AND SOUTH.

This time a year agone I strolled
　　With *Her* beside the sea :
The shores were white—the wind blew cold—
　　The waves were dashing free.

We heeded not the wintry storm.
　　But strolled with even pace ;
Around was gloom—but bright and warm
　　Shone Love's light from her face—

Her young pale face, with eyes so blue.
　　And wreathed with braids of gold.
Its smile so tender and so true—
　　What tho' the day were cold ?

25

And now I wander by the main,
  The Sun is blazing high ;
The waves are laughing as they win
  Its splendour from the sky.

The hills are basking in the glow,
  And from each deep green vale
The orange and the myrtle throw
  Their fragrance on the gale.

But yet methinks yon bleak white shore,
  Beside the Northern Sea—
Yon leaden sky all clouded o'er,
  Were brighter far to me.

THE MAY.

THERE is a fragrance in the air—
   The sun is warm and bright to-day;
And whitening round me everywhere
   I see the May.

The same pure flowers, a month agone,
   I gathered 'neath a bluer sky,
And was not then, as now, alone,
   For Thou wast nigh.

Their clusters are as rich, their flower
   As white, by breeze as balmy tossed:
And yet I've asked myself this hour,
   " What is't they've lost?"

27

They?   Nothing: still their scent they fling
  As sweetly to the wind ; but I ?
I've lost the glory of the Spring
  In heart and eye.

Their life within my Highland Glen
  Is fair as on thy Southern plain ;
But mine amid the ways of men
  Is girt with pain.

Its light and bloom are left with thee,
  Where thou art happy, far away ;
And night and gloom remain with me,
And memory stings me, when I see
  The flowering May.

AT THE EXHIBITION.

SHE trod these galleries and courts :
    And here she paused and gazed—
To landscape bright or sculpture fair
    Her sweet blue eyes upraised :
And here her silk robe rustled past,
    Her airy footstep fell.
As on the rosy summer eve
    The chime of Vesper bell—
She drank the beauty of the scene,
    She knew its thrilling spell.

Her heart, that in the angel sphere
    Of pure Love ever dwelt,
Like star in sky serene and clear,
    The sacred influence felt ;

And at the holy Shrine of Art
  She bowed her reverent head,
And communed with the mighty Soul
  That breathes in quick and Dead.
And felt upon her life the light
  Of the Immortals shed.

And I, who now where once she passed,
  Pass like the mournful breeze
That sighs along an autumn vale,
  Where Spring once decked the trees—
I too can feel my being knit
  To hers more closely now :—
It seems as if I saw once more
  Thought throned upon her brow,
And knelt before her loveliness,
  Where laurelled heads might bow.

It seems as if we 'bode once more
  Within the zone of light,
That gleamed around us long ago,
  Most beautiful and bright ;
As if we met on blessed shores
  Beyond Time's moaning foam—

With plumy palms and summer winds,
  'Neath Heaven's wide sunbright dome,
And angel voices singing low,
  " Fair children, this is home."

Alas! it is a fancy frail,
  And I am far from thee :
Yet thy calm Presence lingers still
  In these fair halls with me.
I gather comfort, for methinks
  These teach this lesson clear—
That with the Lovely, True, and Good
  Thy spirit finds its sphere ;
And that, whene'er these shining ones
  Are round me, Thou art near.

AUTUMNAL.

The sun is sparkling on the frosty braes
And on the shining waters; all the woods
Stand gorgeous in thin robes of red and gold
And orange; the low fields lie stript and still;
And over all the heaven bends keen and blue.
And as I look around, I mark each nook
Where she and I spent unforgotten hours
In rosy summer-time; and now they seem
Most sombre and most lonely; for with me
Her memory abides (but she is gone)
Like a sweet perfume from a hidden shore—
Like a low echo when the harp is still—
Like a meek twilight when the sun is set.
There, 'neath the plane that every now and then

Shivering, shakes off its sere, reluctant leaves,
I sat and read, with low and lingering tone,
Old songs and ballads of our Scottish glens.
Or knightly tales of chivalry and love,
In the soft language of the sunny South :
Whilst 'neath her pencil yon blue ridge of hills
Across the lake rose shadowy on the page.
O'er which bent her fair form and smiling face.
'Neath yonder feathery lime, whose few pale leaves
Still clinging, flutter round its slender sprays,
Hung childhood's pendulous delight—the swing.
Ah ! still I hear her silvery mirthful laugh
The while she flew up to the shadow cool
Of the green branches—then swept rustling back.
Shooting in music and in fragrance through
The air her beauty seemed to fill with light,
And making, Iris-like, a fairy are
Under the deep cool linden, in the noon
Of those dear days of summer.   Where the stream.
With foam-flecked eddies from its channel rough
And flowery marge, shoots bubbling to the loch.
We sat and watched the wavelets as they broke
In glittering gushes on the hard grey sands ;
Or the long rolling lines of flashing light

Rippling along the waters toward the strand ;
Or the white sails that glistened on the deep
Far out to seaward ; or the quivering haze
Through which the villa's white 'mid woodlands green
Round the hot shores gleamed faintly ; or we heard
The even dash of oars, or boisterous cries
Of children playing somewhere by the beach
Borne idly over the sun-sprinkled meer,
And echoed idly back ; and then her voice
Would lose its love-linked music on the air,
That seemed to listen hushed and pleased the while
To tones so soft and clear.   And now—ah me !—
The voice is musical to me no more—
Those fairy feet tread other paths—those eyes
Gaze on far-distant landscapes.   I am left
With but the memory, that can never fade,
Hesper-like, earliest in my nightly sky ;
Phosphor-like, last to dim in garish morn,
When the loud world to toil awakes ;—and she—
Does she remember ?

THE LODGINGS.

SLEEPING, we hardly knew we slept.
  So full of haunted life we seemed ;
  Dreaming, we knew too well we dreamed,
Such stifling horrors o'er us swept.

When longed-for morn illumed the sky,
  Aroused we heard the Street's shrill calls,
  And watched the spiders on the walls,
Or nimbler insects leaping nigh.

Eating, we scarce knew what we ate,
  Disguised in dirt was all our food,
  And e'en when we pronounced it good,
The word of praise came faint and late.

— — — -

Drinking, we shuddered as we drank,
  The lymph was never clear and cold.
  The tumblers wore an aspect old—
The dull carraffes were green and dank.

And up and down and all around
  Black smells possest the sultry air—
  The fiend of smell seemed everywhere
To sit on high enthroned and crowned.

Our windows looked upon the Street—
  The Street gave back a stony blaze,
  And sweltering in the noontide rays
The fishy gutters swelled the heat.

And yet despite discomforts all,
  The five brief days serenely passed :
  And still along my path they cast
A gleam that I would fain recall :

And bid again around me pour
  The light of merry eyes—the tone
  Of happy voices that are gone--
Like waters from a lonely shore.

WHERE ARE YE NOW?

Dim shadows of the happy past,
  I sadly miss you now;
Visions and dreams that faded fast,
Hopes bright, but ah! too fair to last,
  Where are ye now?

Scenes, whose remembrance swells my breast,
  And clouds my furrow'd brow,
Coming, in sorrow's garments dress'd,
To rob the empty heart of rest,
  Where are ye now?

37

Dark eyes, before whose melting gaze
   My heart would yielding bow.
Whose glance spoke more than human praise,
When love approving lent its rays,
   Where are ye now?

Soft hands, which oft I've clasp'd in mine,
   When love's low whisper'd vow
Told me round mine one heart would twine,
As round the oak the fair woodbine,
   Where are ye now?

Dear voices, whose bewitching tone
   Chain'd ear and heart, ah, how
Has your once tuneful music grown
So silent? Whither has it flown?
   Where are ye now?

And thou, more loved than all the rest
   Of the beloved, thou
The brightest. gayest, loveliest, best,
That reigned within this lonely breast,
   Where art thou now?

38

Gone where no more life's weary task
  Can mark the throbbing brow;
Gone where joy wears no heavy mask;
Gone where love reigns. I need not ask,
  Where art thou now?

Scenes, hopes, friends, loves, of early years—
  I miss you sadly now—
Why have ye fled? and why appears
This cold dull cloud of sorrow's tears?
  Where are ye now?

GLENDALOUGH AND THE FORGET-ME-NOT.

GLENDALOUGH! when years have sped
O'er thy heights and o'er thy head,
Leaving still thy gloomy brow
Rugged and unsunned as now—
Wrinkling mine with lines of care,
Scatt'ring snows on youth's swart hair—
Through the lapse of weary years—
With their struggles, doubts, and tears—
Thro' the vista of a life
With its trial, toil, and strife.
How shall then those scenes appear
Which I now esteem so dear?
Shall my heart have ceased to feel
Old loved memories o'er it steal?

Shall it scan each tender link
Severed by cold hands, nor think
Sadly of the happy time
When the love was in its prime,
Which had bound those sweetest ties
Under youth's unclouded skies ?
No : tho' every link be broken,
Still shall live one tiny token,
Which shall say, when storms are nigh—
Smiling from its soft blue eye—
" Oh, remember those bright hours—
Live still in those summer bowers—
Let thy heart among them play,
And again be young and gay ;
Manhood's happiest hours, in sooth,
Are when memory wakens youth."
And shall not the gentle word
In my heart of hearts be heard,
Which it speaks to soothe my lot—
True Love's own " Forget me not ?"
Yes, sweet flower, my heart must be
Close barred 'gainst Love and Sympathy,
Ere with equal pulse it beat
When thy modest buds I greet.

41

Ever wear that darling hue,
Emblem of affection true,
That illumed thy slender stem,
Where yon heights the dark Lake hem :
Where I prest thee to my heart.
Swearing we should never part.
Soon the eye that brightly smiled
On me then—shall o'er the wild
Wastes of sea and desert sands
Smile as sweet in distant lands ;
Still I in my bosom hoard
The dear gift of the adored,
And remember, tho' forgot,
She has said " Forget me not."
Yes, mavourneen. this slight flower
Ne'er shall lose its gentle power
To link my thoughts to thee, where'er
On life's lone sea my bark may steer ;
Again the memories to awake
Of the long day beside the Lake ;
To touch to life the hidden rills,
Whence early love its dew distils ;
And as I feel its power and truth,
I'll bless the love that blest my youth.

THE GLEN.

ABOUT two miles from Weissnichtwo,
　　There is a leafy glade—
A brooklet wimpling through it
　　Makes music in the shade;
No winds disturb its stillness,
　　But breathings cool and mild
Rustle among the leaves and flowers,
　　Like the sighs of a sleeping child:
And sparkling waters trickle
　　Adown the glen's steep sides,
To swell with tiny rills the stream
　　That 'neath the green leaves glides,

43

Oozing from slopes of fern and moss,
  With their refreshful showers.
They shed a brighter tint around
  Upon the grass and flowers.
The foxglove nods most haughtily
  In this sequestered dell—
The fairiest music tinkles faint
  From the trembling heatherbell ;
The primrose, springing by the rock,
  Wears a more lovely hue :
The violet and the hyacinth
  Blush with a deeper blue ;
And there with Love's serenest smile,
  Deep in the shadiest nooks,
Peeps the slight flower whose mild blue eye
  Reflects Love's sweetest looks.
The butterfly flits in the sunbeam,
  And the bees—they hum in the lime,
With a sound like the changeless cadence
  Of a dull unvarying rhyme ;
And the cushat's liquid cooings,
  And the thrush's mellow lay,
Link, as with threads of silver,
  The hours of the long still day.

44

And murmuring there for ever,
  The brooklet is at play.
Far in the glen's recesses
  The rocks rise steep and stark,
And the water 'neath their shadow,
  In its pools lies deep and dark :
Atop the trees grow spreadingly,
  And the wild flowers blossom fair :
But save a scattered tuft below,
  The smooth-worn juts are bare.
Just where a little wooden bridge
  Across the burn is thrown,
The rocks close round a narrow pool,
  Deep, dark, and cold and lone :
There with a clear brown current
  The lustrous waters glide,
And the pebbly floor of green and red
  Gleams through the amber tide.
The fairies—from their silvan haunts,
  Where the acorns drink the dew :
Where the hawthorns in the lap of May
  Their fragrant blossoms strew;
Where the sward is meshed with fairy rings,
  And Elfin strains are beat,

Might bathe their dainty limbs unseen.
 In this remote retreat ;
Or Dian, way-worn from the chase.
 Might cool her weary feet.
There on that little homely bridge
 I saw a lady lean—
Methought all else in blank eclipse
 Was lost—she only seen ;
For years had passed since I saw her last.
 And seas had rolled between.

A REVERIE.

How sitt'st thou in thy lonely hall,
  In these November eves,
Hearing the rain in dreary fall
  Upon the trampled leaves—
Watching the ghastly daylight die
  Along the wintry vale—
'Neath fitful gleams of cloud and sky
  Toss'd by the drifting gale?
Look'st thou upon the streaming rain,
  Out on the windy night,
And dream'st old summer back again
  In all its rosy light?
Or dost thou bid the rattling storm
  Let loose its angriest strife,

47

To mimic, in its wild alarm,
  The tempest of thy life?

How sitt'st thou in thy sombre hall
  In these November eves,
When the rain has stayed its sobbing fall
  Upon the sodden leaves—
When in the gloaming far and grim,
  Between the earth and sky,
The pale moon riseth slow and dim,
  While bleak winds moan and sigh?
Recallest thou a dreamlike hour
  Beside a moonlit sea—
The rocky path—the gathered flower—
  The vow—the bended knee?
Or with no shadow on thy brow,
  Dost thou discard each scene—
Each hour I thrill to think of now,
  As though they ne'er had been?

Here spanning all the raving Forth,
  The heaven is black with night,
Save where athwart the icy North
  Shoot trembling trails of light—

They flicker o'er the looming hills
Dead 'neath their hoods of snow,
But they gleam not where the river fills
The rough deep gulf below ;
The river's sullen voice I hear,
But as I list and gaze,
A low loved tone is in mine ear,
And in mine eyes a haze ;
Methinks I see a sparkling tide
Kissing a foreland fair,
And tones of love on the breezes glide,
And fragrance fills the air.

The dream I dream'd is shattered now,
It may not dawn again ;
Would'st bid the lightning's shivered bough
Wave greenly o'er the glen ?
And thy dream—hath it vanished too ?
And has thy dark eye wept ?
And has thy bosom, warm and true
The sad remembrance kept ?
I know not : I may never know,
For as through life we fare—

To meet, were but awakened woe
　　To thee—to me, despair.
Be calm--oh, calm—on God's own earth
　　How many a stricken breast
Sees fade the Love, and Hope, and Mirth,
　　That once it fond carest,
Ere yet it knew their fleeting worth,
　　And yearned for God's own rest.

REMINISCENCE.

Came a phantom to my pillow,
    Hovering o'er my stormy sleep,
As a Petrel o'er the billow
    When wild winds the surges sweep :
And its cheek was wan and hollow.

    And its eye was strangely bright,
And its glitter seemed to follow
    Far away some angry light.
'Mid the shadows of the night—
Gloomy, cold, and death-like night.

Then my spirit trembled, quailing ;
    And I felt the unshed tears,
As a memory came slow sailing
    Up the dusky tide of years—

Memory of the sunny valley,
  'Mid the hills beside the sea—
Sunshine—music—witty sally,
  And the magic girdling thee,
Whom I never more shall see,
Where the main is dashing free.

And I knew thee wan and wasted,
  Worn with sorrow, scathed by Death ;
Knew the lip, where I had tasted
  Rapture in its balmy breath ;
Knew the breast that, fondly swelling,
  Once had throbbed beside mine own,
When the latest hour was knelling,
  Doom within its iron tone;
For it rent a golden zone—
Rent it—left us lorn and lone.

And that faery zone shall never
  Wind us in its trance again,
But its memory traileth ever,
  Like a worm, across the brain :
When the rain is wildly streaming,
  And the thunder growling deep,

Then my spirit, darkly dreaming
  As the phantoms o'er it sweep,
  Haunted, scowls o'er main and steep,
Billows booming, lightning gleaming
  Round its shadowy pathway leap,
In the horror of its sleep—
Till, affrayed, I wake and weep.

TO BLONDINE ON HER BIRTHDAY.

FAREWELL to sweet seventeen, Blondine.
Farewell to sweet seventeen ;
   When the primroses fade
   In the greenwood shade.
The roses bloom out in their sheen,
   Blondine.

When the sun's strong rays
Lift morn's soft haze,
Forth gleams the broad fair scene, Blondine—
   When the jewel-like rill
   Has glanced from the hill,
It rolls proud banks between, Blondine.

And in champaigns wide
  Its silver tide
Flashing afar is seen,
    Blondine.

Farewell to sweet seventeen, Blondine,
Farewell to sweet seventeen ;
    Your bright young years
    That knew no tears
Are among the things that have been,
    And womanhood now,
    On your calm pale brow,
Beams like the crown of a queen,
    Blondine.

Farewell to sweet seventeen, Blondine,
Farewell to sweet seventeen ;
    When your golden hair
    And hue so fair
Are, too, with the things that have been ;
    May the light of truth
    And the dew of youth
Still glisten in thy blue eyne, Blondine ;

Still may hearts be stirred
By thy gentle word.
And smile so sweet and serene,
    Blondine.

Farewell to sweet seventeen, Blondine.
Farewell to sweet seventeen ;
    So, still more dear,
    Each gliding year
Will make thee to this fond heart, Blondine—
    'Twill still be true
    To her it knew,
When life's young leaves were green,
    Tho' none remain,
    Thro' storm and rain,
For memory sad to glean,
    Blondine!

TO EDITH.

Ah, Edith, with the keen bright eyes, do you remember me,
And that cold and misty evening beside the winter sea,
And the piping of the breezes and dripping of the rain,
And the rough billows rolling in from the bleak northern main?

Ah! Edith, laughing Edith! I've often dreamed since then
That I held your hand, and heard your voice, and watched
    your eyes again ;
And I've wakened from the pleasant dream, to sigh, " would
    she were here
With the merry smile that cheered my heart in the op'ning
    of the year."

Ah! Edith, little Edith ! your heart is young and gay ;
And you know not yet the gnawing care, and "grief that
    maketh grey ; "

57

Long, long, within your heart of hearts that gaiety enshrine.
And let its guileless mirthfulness in those bright glances shine.

For Edith! as thro' life you fare, how smooth soe'er your
track,
You'll find it still, at every step, the sweeter to look back.
And that the only living fount of joy and love and truth
Lies deep 'mid the wild tangled flowers that wreathed your
joyous youth.

And Edith! fairy Edith! amid the toils and pains
That mar and manacle our lives—as slaves are cramped with
chains,
Oh! 'tis most sweet to see a ray of light of purest birth,
A beam of Heaven's own sunshine illume this sordid earth.

Such wast thou, merry Edith—just such a ray to me—
Bright as the first green gleam of land across a weary sea:
And welcome as the vesper-bell on a day of noise and strife—
A chord that sounded passing sweet amid the din of life.

Then Edith, sweetest Edith! still let it blithely fling
Its tender echoes round me—still let my memory cling
To the joyous voice, and sunny smile, and eyes so bright
and clear,
That lighted up the sparkling hours in the op'ning of the year.

TO STELLA.

HE writes to Thee—most fair and bright,
  And in his paltry line
Prattles of Love—presumptuous wight,
  And weds his name to thine.
Well! let him scribble. Did he know
  The magic circling thee,
The youngster could not chatter so
  With phrase so glib and free ;
For when the heart of hearts is stirred
  By such a witching spell,
No human speech can lend the word
  That may its secret tell.
The fancy of an idle hour
  May idle rhymes unfold ;

59

The charm that o'er our life has power
  May not be lightly told.
A smiling lip—a merry brow—
  On these a eyes may rest;
But none can mark the ebb and flow
  Of life's blood in the breast.

TO A. M. D.

ARA BELLA—Altar fair!
  My vows, my worship, all are thine :
Hear me breathe my trembling prayer—
    See me prostrate at thy shrine,
      Where I lay the votive flowers
      Of my peace-forsaken hours.

Mary—named of pensive sorrow!
  Look benignant as I kneel ;
From thy pity let me borrow
    Balm to soothe : say—balm to heal—
      Love's own gift and blessing free
      Dare I never ask of thee?

61

De l'Amour! thy liquid name
  Like a crown befits thy brow ;
Ne'er could Love or Beauty claim
  Fairer, sweeter Queen than thou—
    Queen, whose throne of light is reared
    On a bosom crushed and seared.

TO AMARYLLIS.

METHOUGHT I wandered in a wood
  Where the green shade was calm and cool,
And babbling on in gleeful mood
  Glided the stream from pool to pool;
The sunshine of serenest June
  Upon the golden ripples quivered—
The linnet piped his liquid tune—
  In the low breeze the aspen shivered;
And yet to me the leafy glades
  Seemed laden with a dusky gloom,
As with a winter twilight's shades
  Which the broad sun could not illume;
The warbler's song could not dispel
  The silence of the lonely wood;

The merry sunbeams as they fell
  Seemed but to mock the solitude:
But as I strayed, methought the light
  With rosier radiance filled the air.
The streamlet sparkled diamond-bright
  By one green bower, for thou wast there.
I saw thee wreathed in white attire,
  A rosy chaplet on thy brow;
No knightly bard e'er tuned his lyre
  To sing a Ladye fair as thou.
Around thee seemed the flowers to bloom,
  As tho' they knew a Goddess near—
Each stately vista from the gloom
  Waved its wide arms in sunshine clear.
Down on the golden moss I kneeled,
  Where dimpled light thy fairy feet,
My fainting sense in rapture reeled.

  My heart with lightning pulses beat :
Methought, as in a wizard dream
  The woodland scenes seemed far to fade ;
I recked not of the laughing stream,
  Nor of the flowery sunlit glade ;
I only knew thou wast beside,
  And felt upon my sense and soul

TO AMARYLLIS.

Thy beauty like a silver tide
   In waves of light and music roll.
I humbly knelt, then strove to speak ;
   And raised mine eyes ; the light in thine
Was cold, and on thine angry cheek
   The proud blood mantling blighted mine.
The sombre forest boughs did seem
   Again to droop in shade, and moan
Most mournful in the gloaming gleam.
   And horror wrapt the woodland lone.
I saw Thee go, a vision fair ;
   As Evening's glow from cloudy night
Thou wentest, but my heart shall bear
   For evermore thine image bright.
Alas ! thy maiden heart was free,
   But mine for ever is thy thrall ;
Nor ceases still to roam with thee,
   By silent shore, in festal hall ;
And tho' athwart the future drear
   Thy Beauty's ray no more should gleam,
Thy memory ever calm and clear
   Shall be the Spirit of my Dream.

Fair Lady! who that owned a lyre
   Would fail to tune it at thy hest?
What heart could Helicon inspire,
   If dull to thy request?

But ah! the chords I once could wake
   No longer at my bidding thrill;
And but a few faint echoes break
   Their silence sad and still.

My muse is sunk in slumber deep,
   And only stirred from voiceless rest,
When o'er her pallid brow may sweep
   From out the distant West

Wild winds from forests dark and free.—
  Or when the Southern breezes bring
Day-dreams of golden Italy
  Upon their fragrant wing.

The gray and bitter East to-night
  Blows harsh and shrill.   Draw round the fire:
We'll pledge Thee in a goblet bright.
  But lay aside the lyre.

SERENADE.

Darling, sleep; the stars are twinkling
  On the waters slumbering calm.
And the cool clear air is sprinkling
  All the flowers with dewy balm.
Darling, sleep: see I am keeping
  Vigil 'neath thy latticed nest.
All night long while thou art sleeping.
  I will guard thy peaceful rest :
    Sleep, beloved, sleep.

Now she sleeps: the roses clamber
  O'er the trellis, peeping in.
Clustering round her holy chamber—
  All is dim and still within.

Rippling down her long fair tresses
Rise and fall upon her breast,
Soft her cheek the pillow presses,
Pure dove in her fragrant nest :
Sweetest—now she sleeps.

Darling, wake : the morn is breaking,
Let my watch thy kisses close;
Now the trilling birds are waking,
Opening now the blushing rose.
Rise, my love, the night is dying ;
Gaily o'er the laughing sea
Leaps the day ; the breeze is sighing
At thy casement, dear, for thee :
Rise, sweet-heart, arise.

MOSELLE.

WHERE rolls in silent strength the Rhine
  Neath Ehrenbreitstein's martial steeps.
A gentler stream mid groves of vine
  To join its kingly current sweeps.
From smiling plains of sunny France.
  By flowery mead and bosky dell.
And fields where erst oft gleamed the lance.
  Sparkles and winds the fair Moselle.

I saw the hills of far Lorraine
  Rise o'er these scenes of fruits and flowers.
As evening deepened, and the strain
  Of music stirred the rustic bowers

To dance and song ; far, far away
  The peasants of my people dwell,
Mid toil more hard, mid mirth less gay
  Than those which gladden bright Moselle.

The flowers bloomed freshly ; clusters blue
  Festooned the vines that crown the wave ;
But, tho' thus fair the varied view,
  'Twas memory all its beauty gave ;
For one who strays by shady streams,
  In that green isle I love so well,
Thinks not her presence throngs the dreams,
  That gild the waves of blue Moselle.

Adieu ! dear stream ; I ne'er may gaze
  Upon thy glancing waters more ;
Yet pensive thoughts like Autumn's haze
  Shall ever gather round thy shore ;
And tho' around my struggling bark
  Life's storms may frown and surges swell,
One scene no gloom shall tinge with dark—
  Thy vine-wreathed bosom, calm Moselle.

IN THE GARDENS OF HEIDELBERG CASTLE.

See! athwart the level Rhein-gau slowly rolls the purple haze,
As toward the far-blue Vosges sinks the day-god's slanting blaze,
Through the darkly-louring fortress, which the cloud-charged
    winds have piled
See him burst, as through primeval forests flames in fury wild:
See his rays like fiery sabres flashing 'mid a routed host,
Then like golden wavelets streaming outward to a viewless coast—
Outward o'er an azure ocean slumbering in eternal calm,
Where the happy spirits wander 'mid their tranquil isles of palm.
Now all bathed in blood-red splendour, like a hero from a fight,
Proudly has the orb descended to the swarthy arms of night;
She has kiss'd his sultry forehead with her dewy lips and cool,
And has laid him down to slumber on her bosom soft and full,
And the silvery moon has risen, and upon the earth has smiled

Softly, as a youthful mother bends to kiss her sleeping child,
Still above the Holy Mountain floats a wreath of lustre faint,
Like a pale and waning glory round the brow of dying saint:
And I muse, the while I watch it fading into twilight grey,
How the unseen western heaven still is bright with rosy day;
How, the while the dews are falling on the myrtle and the vine,
And a fitful ghost-like shadow broods above the haunted Rhine.
Far away, o'er chequer'd landscapes, rapid river, cold grey shore,
Woody glens and waving uplands, rugged mountains wild and hoar,
Still the day in mellow glory lingers soft by moor and glade,
Struggling, as it slowly parteth, to repel th' advancing shade.
Softly o'er the fells of Scotland—softly o'er green Erin's plains—
Does the dewy gloaming gather, as the orb of glory wanes:
Softly from the dimpled ocean comes the gently-breathing air,
Sighing 'mid the solemn woodlands softly as a lisped prayer.
Ah! methinks I hear its music stealing like a vesper-hymn,
As though guardian angels bore it hither through the shadows dim,
Mingling with it loving voices seem my exiled heart to thrill:
Hark! my name is fondly whispered. Yes! I am remembered still!

COLOGNE.

Oh, town of mingled fumes and stenches,
Of unwash'd children, ugly wenches,
And jabberers whose broken French is
    Mix'd up with rough-shod German!
Against your stinking streets and lanes,
High-priced hotels, unfinished fanes,
Your gurgling gutters, yawning drains,
    Well could I preach a sermon.
Had men but courage 'mid this scent
To give their sicken'd anger vent,
They soon would force you to repent.
    Worse than Augean stable!
But none for more than half a day
In such a nauseous hole can stay;
They see the sights—the bills they pay—
    And bolt as hard's they're able.

74

RHINE WINE.

WINE from the vine
By the castled Rhine,
Oh ! what a magic spell is thine :
As the broad river joyously boundeth—
As its billow note ever gleefully soundeth.
So thy bright wavelets spring,
While our tall goblets ring,
And chiming round them fling
Music and mirth divine—
Rhine—Father Rhine !

Stint not the stream,
Let its genial beam
Like the crimson flash of the ruby gleam :

Like the blue eyed flowers that Love lets not perish,
Those too fleeting hours let Memory cherish,
    When o'er the misty plain
    We've watched the daylight wane,
    While the gay flask we drain—
        Bright with thy best sunshine,
        Rhine—Father Rhine!

    Wine from the vine
    By the royal Rhine,
    A long farewell to thy spell benign!
Bold Fatherland—proudly crowned River!
Broad plain—vine-wreathed strand, I leave ye for ever:
    Yet under distant skies,
    Chill, but for love-lit eyes,
    Oft shall your memory rise.
        Thy vineyards, pleasure's shrine,
        Rhine—Father Rhine!

A VOICE FROM NAPLES UNDER BOMBA.

Powers! that rule the fates of nations
  And the patriot's labours bless,
Loose your lightnings on the tyrant;
  Let his fall be our redress.
Let a glorious sun uprising
  Sweep the shadows from our brow;
May the bonds no more disgrace us.
  Under which we're writhing now.
Ours be noontide's Orient splendour.
  His the murkiest midnight's gloom,
Ours the joy. the feast, the gladness.
  His the woe and curse and doom.
Ours the plenty, ours the riches.
  His the penury and dole,

Ours high Heaven's choicest blessing,
  His the blight that sears the soul.
Ours to draw the gaze of nations,
  Who admiring see us rise,
Like the dawn on Eastern landscapes,
  Like the moon in summer skies :
His to fall mid shame and loathing,
  Mid a people's jeer and hiss.
To the foulest pit of darkness
  In the fathomless abyss :
Ours to soar from high to higher,
  His to sink from worse to worse ;
Ours to know life's mirth and blessing,
  His to dree its weariest curse.
May his rooftree shiver round him,
  May the night of darkness fall,
May the grimmest memories haunt him,
  May the blackest dreams appal :
May the minions of his glory
  And the slaves of his renown
Turn upon him now to curse him,
  And to drag his honour down.
May his children, whining vagrants,
  Beg their coarse and scanty meal,

May they meet with hands of iron.
　And with bosoms cold and steel.
May the heart that shared his fortune
　Leave him in his ruin now.
May he wander shunned and spit at.
　With God's curse-stamp on his brow:
Then great God that rulest nations.
　Hear the prayer we pray to thee.—
Deal the Despot his damnation.
　Set thy poor oppressèd free.

EMIGRANTS' SONG.

FAREWELL, ye bold mountains, on whose purple heather
  We've watched the gay sunbeams as richly they shone:
Farewell, dearest glen, where we all lived together,
  Less bonnie thou'lt be when we Exiles are gone.
Dear old land of our fathers we leave thee for ever,
  No more shall we tread on thy grey rocky shore,
Farewell, ye green uplands! thou beautiful River,
  We return—we return—we return no more.

Farewell to the Hills, where as children we roaming
  Have spent happy days in each pine-covered glade,
Never leaving our sports till the grey of the gloaming
  Wrapt mountain and valley and streamlet in shade.

Farewell to the Mother who called me her Dearie,
And oh, may I follow where she's gone before!
But to the bright ingle that once was so cheery,
We return—we return—we return no more.

And farewell to Him—the reverend the hoary,
With his kind smile for virtue, his sad frown for sin,
Who pointed the way, while he told us of glory,
And opening Life's narrow gate, beckoned us in.
Farewell to the Kirk where we prayed with our fathers,
Ah! dear to my heart was its humble bit door,
Small and sad is the number that round it now gathers;
We return—we return—we return no more.

Farewell to the graves where our kindred are lying,
All resting together 'neath Scotia's green sod;
But we Emigrants—we, when we come to be dying,
Will be far from the Land that our forefathers trod.
Farewell ye true Hearts—ye poor sons of the Highlands,
Opprest and forgotten—your state we deplore;
Oh, stay while ye may by your own rugged Islands,
We return—we return—we return no more.

THE BONES OF BRUCE.

Stay!—'twas there they laid King Robert,
  When his soul had rest in God,
Where the holy altar's censers
  Wav'd their incense sweet abroad;
Where the wreath'd and gorgeous mullions
  Shed their twilight of rich rays,
And the choral strain of voices
  Swelled the lofty song of praise :—
And 'twas there we found his ashes
  In their mouldering shroud of gold,
When the blight of careless ages
  O'er the sacred tomb had roll'd ;
When the sunken shafts and arches
  Strew'd the cloisters cold and dim.

82

And around the shatter'd altar,
  Peal'd no more the vesper hymn.

'Twas November's dreary winter,
  And a morn of misty gloom
Wrapp'd the grey and lonely abbey,
  As we gather'd round the tomb :
There within the crumbling coffin,
  'Mid the clammy mould and stones,
In their earth-stain'd tatter'd cerement
  Lay the white and wasted bones.
From the dismal vault we raised them ;
  Long we stood a silent ring,
Gazing on these grisly relics
  Of the great and goodly King :
Albyn's own Immortal Hero,
  Once her bulwark, still her pride,
As when erst he spread the terror
  Of her vengeance far and wide.
Oft of old the headlong onset
  Saw the Southron squadrons reel,
When that arm was seen to brandish
  In the van its deadly steel :

83   G 2

Keen within that hollow socket
   Once had gleam'd his lightning eye.
As he watched the midnight beacon
   Redd'ning 'neath the Scottish sky ;
Flashing with the fire of glory,
   Oft it scanned the stubborn fight.
While adown the breeze of battle
   Rang,—" St. Andrew and our Right !"

What though now through roofless ruins
   Rain and sleet his tomb defile,
And the fitful blasts of winter
   Howl along the darken'd aisle ;
What though now the solemn wailing
   Of his dirge be heard no more,
And the night-owl's hooting only
   Echo through the arches hoar—
We could see the sky of summer
   Radiant with serenest light,
While the mighty God of battles,
   Bore the hero through the fight :
We could see the Lion standard,
   Proudly waving o'er the Free,

While the stream through all its mazes,
　　Crimson foaming sought the sea ;
We could see the gory casket,
　　On the stricken field of Spain,
Scotland's royal heart enshrining,
　　'Mid the heaps of Paynim slain ;
Ay, and we could see him resting,
　　In his still and stately sleep—
O'er his corse his glory beaming
　　Like the moonlight o'er the deep.

Calmly rest thou great departed;
　　Guard, ye hoary towers, his dust ;
Never on your holiest altars
　　'Shrined ye such a sacred trust.

Albyn's Hero ! though the ages
　　Haste along their fiery range—
Though the strife of selfish factions,
　　And the din of weary change,
Fain would banish from our bosoms
　　All the glorious days of old—
Though the curse of Mammon fetters
　　Hearts whose faith is dim and cold—

85

Though the stern and headlong Present
    Heeds not the majestic Past,
The remembrance of thy glory
    Changeless in our hearts shall last :
Still thy deathless fame shall fire us,
    And the land that holds thy grave
Still shall be the tyrant's terror,
    The Avenger of the slave :
And our proud embanner'd Lion,
    Borne aloft of yore by thee,
Still shall ramp its grim defiance
    O'er the Faithful, Brave, and Free.

DALHOUSIE.

THEY tell us that our age is weak in faith,
In action unheroic ; that the prize
Men struggle for is not the proud award
Of conscience smiling on a lofty deed—
But place, or power, or gold, or vulgar fame,
Whose hollow baubles catch the common eye,
That pierces not beyond the rough-grained husk,
Into the secret life of men and things.
Too true : the mighty Spirit that upheld
The world's grand heroes in their life-long wars
With falsehood and oppression and brute force ;
That sent them forth to wrestle in the field,
Or die amid the bigot's fires, or pine
In low damp dungeons bound in tyrant's gyves,

Is rare amongst us, and the very name
Of Hero laid aside for want of use.
But still men's hearts are generous and just,
And still, when some bold deed or thought stands forth
Above th' ignoble level of the times,
Like a tall rock above a misty sea,
With an electric sympathy they thrill
With one strong throb of reverence for the good,
Of homage for the faithful—brave and true.
So, when of late we heard the moving tale,
How he, who had so long the sceptre swayed
Of our majestic Empire of the East,
Had, worn and weary, laid the sceptre down.
All hearts in Britain—save a sorry few
Barred to all noble influence—leapt with pride,
For we remembered how, eight weary years,
In peace and war—amid contending broils—
Harassed by care—deafened with clamorous cries
Of right and wrong—with sorrow oft at heart—
And the unceasing toil of anxious thought
Tasking his mind's activity—he had,
Careless of calumny or glozing praise,
Done what he deemed his duty—with few words,
And no parade, but with resistless strength

Of energy and purpose—so that he
Had bent to his strong will with stern control
All elements antagonistic, and
Left on broad India's destiny the stamp
Of his own lofty genius, and the law
He made his guide, of justice, truth, and right.
And wisdom stretching out a hand to grasp
Its treasures from the future: and we said,
As with one voice, " Here is indeed a hero !—
One who, forgetting self, and all the cares
That make the paltry lives of paltry men,
Used to their utmost all the noble powers
Bestowed by God, to spread God's blessed boons
Of enterprise, and wealth, and peacefulness,
Of gentler manners, purer modes of life,
And heartier reverence for law and right."
Yes ; and in after years, when one shall ask,
As 'mid the splendours of that gorgeous clime,
He sees how some great mind has been at work,
Unfettering the native powers of men ;
Unfolding the resources lying hid
Beneath the dust of ages, or the gloom
Of tropic forests, or the barren reign
Of ignorance and sloth and apathy—

" Who first began these renovating toils,
Creating out of anarchy and death,
Order and fruitful life ?" With one glad voice,
India shall answer—" 'Twas the Scottish Lord,
Who, in the days of good Victoria,
Came hither, and for eight bright years maintained
A rigid, upright, honourable rule,
Swaying the sceptre like a crowned King,
Above corruption and above reproach;
Sweeping away the errors of the past,
And looking far adown the stream of years
To mark the channel where erewhile would roll
The mighty tide of our prosperity.
So all men honoured him ; and when at length
The day had come when he must leave our shore,
The cannon thundered and the trumpets rang,
And crowds prest round him, to have one last look
Of their Queen's king'y Viceroy ; when they tried
To raise a hearty cheer, and cry ' God speed '
Their voices failed them, and they died away
To a low sob of sorrow, for their hearts
Were swelling high with great and mournful thoughts,
As they beheld him, pale and worn and weak
With the great burden he so well had borne,

And bearing, for all others lighter made,
Yet with a steadfast purpose in his eye
Which told that in the enfeebled frame there dwelt
A spirit dauntless and unwearied yet,
And nerved like a bent bow for other toil,
If duty should demand new sacrifice.
He left us for his home in that far isle
Which, like a beacon in a wintry sea,
To all the storm-tost is the star of hope.
But here he left an unforgotten name—
A monument no time can overthrow—
The mem'ry of those eight heroic years,
A heritage to us—to all who love
Faith, honour, wisdom, and unflinching will."

THE LEGEND OF S. JULIAN.

I.

THE Knights hold revel in the hall,
    Hark to the music pealing—
Within. before the holy Rood
    The aged Priest is kneeling.
The Baron bold amid his peers
    The joyous hour is keeping—
The Lady, o'er her new-born babe,
    A mother's tears is weeping.
The towers are old—the vassals bold,
    The lands are broad and fair ;
Then let the red wine circle free,
    To hail the lordly heir.

II.

The soft west wind was blowing faint.
　　O'er rose and violet playing ;
And up the valley all alone,
　　Was young Lord Julian straying.
He thought upon his mother's love,
　　And on his father's pride,
When he was 'ware of a gloomy shade,
　　And a presence at his side :
" Ha ! think'st thou of thy mother's love,
　　Feel'st thou her soft caressing ?
Ha ! deem'st thou thou'rt thy father's pride,
　　The child of hope and blessing ?
There's father's blood upon thine hand—
　　And doom shall haunt thy way—
They hailed thy birth with mickle mirth,
　　They yet shall curse the day."

III.

The evening fell—the red light died
　　Along the castle wall ;
They set the goblets on the board,
　　The torches in the Hall.

93

The shadows from among the hills
   O'er moor and grove were creeping,
And the lady, at her lattice high,
   A fretful watch was keeping;
The warder stood without the gate,
   The anxious sire beside him—
" The night is mirk, and full of storm—
   God grant no ill betide him!"
The whole night long an eager throng
   Await his home returning;
And watchmen shout, and bells ring out,
   And beacon fires are burning.
Day broke—but Julian never came;
   And thro' the lonely years
He came not, and his mother wept
   A childless mother's tears;
And his father never more rode forth
   Amid his knightly peers.

IV.

And where was he, the gallant boy,
   The heir of the gallant race?
Oh! flying far by cliff and scar,
   Like the stag in the deadly chase.

With cheek blanched white in the stormy night,
   And dumb fear at heart he fled,
And ever he deemed that he heard behind
   A close and tireless tread.
The night went by, and the sullen sky
   Gleamed forth into rosy day,
But still he fled, in his nameless dread,
   Along the dreary way,
For he deemed that Satan came hard behind,
   To make his soul his prey.
At last, when many a day was gone,
   He climbed a mountain crest—
Beneath him rolled a great wide sea,
   The sunlight on its breast,
And by the shore a meadow green,
   A meadow full of rest ;
And on a cliff beside the sea
   There stood an ancient keep,
Whose banner with a rose red Cross
   Waved proudly o'er the deep.
" My mother and my sire," said he,
   " I ne'er may see again ;
'Gainst yonder whisper of the fiend
   I steel my heart in vain,

Even now methinks I see my hand
  Red with the damning stain ;
Ah ! heavy hearts are theirs, I ween,
  And mine is sad and sore :
But Satan's guile would work us woe,
  Were I to see them more ;
I'll tarry with this Christian Knight.
  Beside this pleasant shore."

V.

The years rolled on, and Julian dwelt
  Hard by the Northern Sea.
In battle's brunt—in council hall
  Was none renowned as he ;
No friend but loved—no foe but feared
  To hear Lord Julian's name ;
And so he moved among his peers.
  A Knight of mickle fame :
Yet Fame's is but a barren voice,
  Unless its echoes blend
With a soft low music sweeter far
  Than tones of friendliest friend.
That sings alike mid pomp and pride,
  Mid downfall and distress.

" Beloved, I cannot love thee more,
  I do not love thee less."
Ah! she was fair with sunny hair,
  And eyes like violets blue,
And her cheeks like roses blushing faint
  Mid lilies sprent with dew,
As Julian drew her to his heart
  Within her trellised bower,
And she chode him not as he told his love,
  At twilight's witching hour,
As they knelt to plight their lifelong troth,
  Before the altar fair,
The priest, I ween, had never seen
  So beautiful a pair.

VI.

My masters—'tis a heavy tale
  Ye ask me to rehearse—
For I must tell how Satan's wiles
  Smote Julian with a curse.
The envious fiend, with scowl malign,
  Surveyed his princely state,
Then turned him to his darkest den,
  To weave his web of hate.

Clad as a palmer grey, he passed
 Along the valley fair,
Where first his words struck Julian's heart
 With horror and despair.
He passed beside the castle gate,
 Where stood an aged dame—
Ah! still the mother's heart beat young
 At sound of Julian's name;
She saw not in the evil eye,
 The spark of fiendish flame.
"Thy son that left thee long ago,
 Is now a famous Knight;
Away to North his flag flies forth,
 Above his castled height,
And a lovely lady fills his halls
 With music, love, and light."

VII.

The sun had sunken broad and red
 Beneath the ocean's rim,
And thro' the evening mist, the towers
 Soared upwards vast and dim:
The Lady for her Lord's return
 Is watching in the Hall—

'Tis not his step that falls without,
  'Tis not his tones that call ;
Two aged travellers enter in,
  " Fair daughter—ere we die,
God wills that we should see the boy
  We lost in years gone by.
The holy man who bade us forth
  Said Christ would be our guide ;
Until we saw his banner flaunt,
  Where rolled the northern tide :
Now this we deem is Julian's home,
  And thou art Julian's bride ?"

VIII.

Ah me ! the dream of many years—
  The hope that had outlasted
So many shocks—so many fears—
  In one wild moment blasted !
He comes from cares of war and state,
  Worn with the long day's toil—
Yearning to hear the one sweet voice,
  To see the one sweet smile.
Weary of council and of court,
  Weary of sword and crest,

Weary of every thought, save this—
  "My loved one loves me best,"
He comes, and seeks the inmost hall,
  Where she has bade them rest.
Alack, what cursed Fate had doomed
  This night he should not meet
The welcomer, who ne'er had failed
  Till now his step to greet ?
A dim surmise of evil touched
  A chord of nameless fear—
" Why comes she not ?   It was her wont
  To hail my coming—here."
He drew the curtain 'neath whose folds
  He first had clasped his bride,
Within there lay a bearded man.
  A woman by his side.
There fell on him the utter woe
  Of love and faith betrayed—
Then like a flood the wild deep rage
  Burst forth—he clasped his blade,
And once, and twice, and once again,
  He dealt the furious blow—
The blood is pouring red and fast.
  The moan is faint and low :

Then resting on his gory sword,
  Stung thro' with woe and hate,
A dull dumb horror shakes his soul,
  He knows his sire too late ;
A murderer now—the hellish fiend
  Has wrought his cursed fate.

IX.

Within a sunlit southern vale
  I heard the tale I tell,
From a holy hermit who abode
  Within a lonesome cell ;
His robe was rough—his feet were bare—
  His cheek with fasting wan,
A wasting sorrow marred his face,
  Albeit a holy man.
"Father," I said, "what woe is thine
  That thus has crossed thy brow ?"
A sudden shudder wrung his frame—
  Methinks I see him now :
"These hands—these withered hands," said he.
  "A father's blood have spilt—
Here wasted with my life-long woe
  I expiate my guilt."

"And *She?*" I said—for well I knew
  There lurked as sore a grief
As that for which in utterance
  His soul had sought relief.
"And *She?*" I said—I scarce could frame
  The words I sought to speak ;
A tear from Sorrow's deepest fount
  Rolled down his haggard cheek :
"Where stood my castle in the north,
  Rises a cloister gray ;
There for my father's soul and mine
  The holy sisters pray,
And there the saint that was my bride
  Remembers me alway."

       X.

No more—my masters, 'tis a tale
  Ye well may ponder long,
For seldom is so stern a rede
  Woven in the web of song.
Beware Him who can fool the wise,
  Who can undo the strong.

THE CAUDINE FORKS.

A ROMAN BALLAD.

I.

'Twas since we built our city
  Four hundred years and more,
When to our walls the Samnites
  A flag of treaty bore ;
But proudly scorned the Fathers
  To treaty to accede,
While yet the Roman army
  For Rome and them could bleed.

II.

To Samnium the heralds
  Have hied them back from Rome.

And told their heavy tidings
　　To the warriors at home:
Then up rose Caius Pontius,
　　Their leader tried and true,
Who aye had a stout heart to dare
　　And a strong hand to do:
" The Gods who live for ever,
　　Who bless the patriots' pain,
Upon our deeds are smiling,
　　And will our cause maintain.
But on the haughty Romans
　　Their angry frown is bent,
Who to unyielding enmity
　　Have long resentment lent,
Who would not hear our offers
　　Of Peace and of amends,
And arrogant refused to join
　　With us, as friends with friends:
If this wolf-suckled brood of thieves,
　　Implacable and fierce,
With swords that long to stream with blood,
　　And spears that thirst to pierce,
Must plant their fangs in honest breasts,
　　Must spread the sway of Rome,

Must trample on our Samnite hearths,
    Then boldly bid them come ;
But we who fight for freedom,
    For Truth—for Right—for Laws—
Beloved Fatherland, for Thee,
    Have aye the strongest cause."
He said,—and from his hearers
    A mighty shout arose,
" To arms !—to arms !—bold Pontius,
    We burn to meet the foes ;
We long in those proud Roman hearts
    To blunt our Samnite steel,
And since our friendship they have scorned,
    Our vengeance let them feel !"
So forth he marched his army,
    And close in ambush lay,
Where Caudium's rugged rocks and glens
    Hem in the darkling way.

III.

Beguiled by crafty rumours,
    Which cunning falsehood spread,
In an evil hour the Roman Chiefs
    Their forces onward led ;

105

To penetrate the Caudine Forks,
　Where o'er the narrow path
Dark cliffs and precipices frown,
And thick rough woods with shadow brown
　Cast gloom and mutter wrath.
But nought the Romans dreaded,
　Proud gleamed each eagle eye,
And quicker throbbed each bosom
　To think the combat nigh ;
And lightly pressed each footstep,
　Each helm and shield glanced bright,
And on the spear-points of the brave
　The sun flashed glorious light :
On marched the noble army,
　Down thro' the deep defile,
And pennons flutter in the breeze,
　And trumpets sound the while :
Loud clangs the martial music,
　The horses prance and neigh,
As eager to the fight to rush,
To struggle thro' the madd'ning crush
　And tumult of the fray ;
And so along the fatal vale
　Moved on the brave array.

Anon beyond the level mead
   The farther gorge they reach,
Then chill dismay crept o'er them,
   And hushed gay laugh and speech :
The way was barred with rocks and trees,
   And high piled barricades ;
And in the dusky glen beyond
   Amid its horrent shades
Anon a spear would glitter,
   A brazen shield would clank.
Anon a jeering laugh would rise ;
   And in our host Hope sank,
As sinks in a tempestuous night,
When clouds are low and waves are white
And sky and sea their rage unite,
   The seaman's only plank.
Back to the Pass behind them,
   Wherethro' they marched before.
They sped, half hoping they might yet
   Its narrow gorge explore ;
But Samnite guile had guarded
   Against escapement there.
And barricades and armed men,
Thronging the entrance to the glen.
   Complete the cursed snare.

IV.

No captain's voice was needed
　　Their footsteps to arrest,
For stupifying horror
　　Had seized each manful breast :
In all their souls was anguish,
　　That sought no voice in words ;
They looked down at their shining greaves,
　　And griped their glittering swords,
And drew their helmets closer
　　O'er their brow's knotted veins,
And the horsemen on their sullen steeds
　　Let fall the useless reins :
Low drooped the lazy pennons.
　　That waved erewhile so gay ;
No note of trump or clarion stirred,
　　But in the silence loud was heard.
　　The babbling brook at play.

V.

Oft in the gloom of winter,
　　When the ice the streams had bound.
And leaden skies looked cheerlessly
　　Upon the cheerless ground ;

Oft, when the sultry Dogstar
  Blazed in the copper sky,
And all that lived shrank withered
  From the glare of his fiery eye;
Oft when the sickly Autumn
  With fever's stifling breath,
And noxious damps and vapours
  Had scattered pain and death;
Oft when by staring ruin
  In hours of dread assailed,
When prospects were the darkest.
  Those hearts had never quailed.
Which now, when through that silence
  The Samnite laughter rung,
Like the mirth of mocking demons
  Were like a bow unstrung;
And the tear of rage and shame and grief
  Which Pride disdains to shed,
But which will sometimes from the eye
  Drop like a tear of lead,
'Neath many an eyelid gathered.
  As grimly they survey
The foe—the crag encircled plain—
The heights they'd give a world to gain.

The ruddy clouds that marked the wane
    Of the ill-omened day.

VI.

Night drew her mantle o'er them
    Bewailing still their fate,
Each voice was raised in sorrow,
    None spake in cool debate :
Through the long hours of watching,
    You might have heard one say,
" Let's burst thro' every barrier
    That blocks our onward way,
And let our blood roll down the glen
    Ere comes the morning grey."
Another—" While these mountains
    Still raise their woody crown—
While these black woods above us
    Still throw their shadows down :
How can we reach the Samnites
    Perched on the craggy height ?
In vain is all our valour,
    In vain our Roman might :
Like mangy hounds in kennel,
    When the pack is full in cry.

Or like a hooded falcon,
When the trembling game is nigh—
We here must lie inactive,
Nor raise our battle shout,
And see the star of victory
Shine on yon dastard rout."

VII.

Oft when the dewy twilight
Falls softly, and the haze,
The cool grey vapours gather,
Rises where Tiber strays,
When 'neath the verdant vine leaves
That shade his cottage door,
The veteran sits recalling
The stirring times of yore—
When from the sloping pastures
The lowing herds return,
And cheerily the twinkling lamps
Within the lattice burn ;
When from the rich Campagna
The sounds of laughter ring,
As the treasures of the vineyards
The peasants homeward bring :

When the light tinkling music
  Tells you that nimble feet
Are bounding in the merry dance,
  Or when the distant bleat,
From some sequestered sheepfold
  Upon the purple hill,
Is heard to echo fairily
  With the prattle of the rill;
Then, round the old man's threshold
  The groups of rustics meet,
The old men standing round him,
  The children at his feet,
The blacksmith from his anvil,
  With his apron on his arm;
The sturdy hind who guides the plough
  Along the smiling farm ;
The herdsman from the valley,
  With his flageolet and crook ;
The fisher with his rod and line,
  Wet from the brawling brook ;
All gather round expectant
  To hear the old man tell
Of how this town was taken,
  Of how that hero fell ;

Of how the Etruscan wavered,
    Or Volsci's squadrons reeled
When the fierce Roman war-cry
    Swept wildly o'er the field :
But his lip would quiver angrily,
    And his brow grow black with rage,
And vindictive fires would glitter
    In eyes undimmed by age,
When the spectre hand of memory
    Would bring before his sight
The horror and the weary length
    Of that, the Caudine night.

VIII.

When calls the clanging trumpet
    The Legions to the field,
And fires that quenchless valour
    That ne'er was known to yield ;
When on their shores invading
    They see the Punic fleet,
Bearing the might of Carthage,
    The might of Rome to meet :
The thought of hated Caudium
    Nerves every arm to fight—

113

Gives to each hand a triple strength.
A more than Roman might—
Gives a wild inward lightning
To every flashing eye,
That glitters with a demon gleam
When the dread hour draws nigh :
Then to the murderous onset
They rush with headlong charge ;
In vain the stalwart foemen
Oppose the spear and targe ;
As 'neath the wintry whirlwind
Totters the lofty pine,
When blast on blast comes sweeping
Thro' the glens of Apennine :
As in the surfs of Adria,
Before the howling gale,
The vessel flies 'neath murky skies
With shivered mast and sail :
So on the scene of combat
The mangled squadrons yield.
As the legions pouncing on their prey,
Their eagles soaring o'er the fray.
With furious onslaught sweep away
The enemy from the field.

IX.

And since that coward insult
    That stained their spotless fame,
No blot has ever fallen
    Upon the Roman name;
And now in all Italia
    No name is known like theirs,
'Mid all its subject Provinces
    None such high honour bears.
Where in the sunny valleys
    Of Sicily's gay isle,
The shepherd's lute and dance and song
    The careless hours beguile;
Where hang the nest-like hamlets
    Among the woody steeps,
And down the sides of Apennine
    The snow-white torrent leaps;
Where in the fruitful meadows
    Bathed by the dark blue seas
The fisher's cottage glimmers white
    Beneath the umbrageous trees;
Along that coast where Naples
    Shines by its lordly Bay,

Where Tiber rolls by Ostia,
   Where Anxur's wavelets play ;
From where Tarentum's harbours
   Their thousand barks enclose.
To where thro' old Etruria
   The winding Arno flows ;
From the gay southern gardens,
   Up that enchanted shore
Laved by the Adrian waters,
   To where the mountain's hoar
Hide in their hollow valleys
   The rude Helvetian's home,
No name is whispered with such fear
   As the proud name of Rome.

Supposed to be recited some time in the period between the conquest of Samnium and the close of the Punic Wars.

IN MEMORIAM M. H. M.

Here rests in Christ, until He come again,
One o'er whose ashes Love hath shed such tears
As only Truth and Piety and Love
Can claim from hearts sore-stricken. Who would trace
On this cold stone her virtues' elegy,
When in a thousand breasts Love's hand hath writ,
As deep as life, her name and memory?
For all revered and loved her. She was one
To whom the young and old—the rich and poor—
Could come in brightest or in darkest hours,
And find a friend whose smile would deepen joy,
Whose gentle word would soothe the pang of grief—
Who loved all, sympathized with all, because
Her heart was full of Christ—the fount of Love.

117

And here she lived thus worthily : her life
Encircled with the light of deeds and words
That made the dark rough world around her brighter ;
Until it pleased her God with summons swift
To call her Spirit to its home in Heaven,
To await the morn that shall make all things new.

MORNING HYMN.

Thou who slumb'rest not nor sleepest,
Thou who vigil o'er us keepest,
Bending from thy nightless heaven,
Thy beloved's sleep hast given.

Lord, the dayspring from on high
Brightens in the eastern sky ;
At the threshold of the day,
For thy strength and grace I pray.

As the shadows upward roll,
Chase all darkness from my soul ;
Like the lily's glistening dew,
Purity and joy renew.

Leave me not, dear Christ, this day ;
Cheer mine heart. and smoothe my way ;
Let me lean upon thine arm.
Safe from peril and alarm.

May thy peace possess my mind ;
May my works thy favour find ;
  oy or grief—whate'er betide—
Draw me nearer to thy side.

Evermore, upheld by Thee,
Let thy love my portion be,
While I tread the pathway bright
Lost at length in perfect light.

EVENING HYMN.

(From the " Thesaurus Hymnologicus.")

Thou, dear Christ, our Light and Day,
Foldest round us evening grey :
Light of light ! in loneliest gloom
Thou the darkness canst illume.

Blessed Lord, this night be near :
Shield from ill, and pain, and fear :
As the hours glide silently,
Grant thy servants rest in Thee.

Let our slumber softly fall;
Let no evil dream appal ;
Suffer not unruly sense
Through our sleep to work offence.

121

Though our eyes be closed in sleep,
May our hearts a vigil keep,
While thy arm is stretched above
Us, the children of thy love.

Christ, our guardian, on us look ;
Every lurking foe rebuke ;
By thy watching and thy pain,
Saviour ! keep our souls from stain.

Lord ! thy servants, poor and frail,
Pray thy grace may never fail ;
If we wake, or if we sleep,
Soul and body bless and keep.

THE END.

www.ingramcontent.com/pod-product-compliance
Lightning Source LLC
Chambersburg PA
CBHW060245030726
47493CB00025B/2324